THE ADVENTURESS

ONE VIRTUE AND A THOUSAND CRIMES
BOOK ONE

MIRÀ KANEHL

Self-publishing author publication. Hochleiten 16, 93455 Traitsching, Germany.

www.mira-kanehl.com

For permissions contact: author@mira-kanehl.com

Cover image by Mirà Kanehl, (C) Canva

First edition, 2018

ISBN: 978-1-386912-75-0 eBook / 978-3-947722-08-2 and 978-3-947722-06-8 and 979-8-224789-70-2 and 978-3-947722-12-9 paperbacks

CONTENTS

FOREWORD

This is a novelette; a brief introduction to the characters and setting. If you enjoy it, the links to follow-up novels are in the back of the book for you.

EPIGRAPH

"A man does what he must—in spite of personal consequences, in spite of obstacles and dangers and pressures—and that is the basis of all human morality."
    –Winston Churchill

CHAPTER 1

A QUESTION OF PRUDENCE

ew Orleans, March 1813

"It will not go unnoticed for much longer, Jean," Mr. Clark said, storming into the dusty attic.

Jean heaved the sack of coffee off his back and onto the splintered shelf with a thump. "What?"

"We must limit using the Lafourche route." He gestured to the sacks of contraband—filled with coffee, sugar and linen—laying at the trapdoor. "Please, Jean, don't parade the streets with the loot. The rumors around the Baratarians are becoming preposterous."

Jean wiped his forehead with his sleeve, the coarse linen and dust scratching his sweaty skin. Theories about the happenings at Barataria, the little island sheltering the Barataria Bay from the Gulf of Mexico, crossed many lips in New Orleans. The officials were busy with the aftermath of the war, so Barataria served as the perfect haven for Jean and his brother Pierre's business. The rumors convinced many people Jean had established his own government there, with reports of three hundred Frenchmen fortified and fourteen cannons in place to ward off intruders. It was a blatant exaggeration, of course, but it kept snoops away.

Mr. Clark cleared his throat. "Prudence is posing a threat."

"That anonymous writer?" Jean scratched the back of his head, staring into the dust on the floorboards where tiny paw prints disappeared in the corner.

"Indeed."

"Ough." Jean discarded Mr. Clark's concern with a swing of the hand, scaring off a fly passing him that buzzed to a window and bumped into it. "Half of what he writes is nonsense." Jean's gaze followed the trapped insect and the dead flies and moths that lay on the windowsill below it.

"The public does not know this."

Jean inhaled the grassy scent of green coffee overpowering that of the dust swirling in the beams of light entering by the two long windows looking onto the street. The wooden floor of the warehouse over Jean's blacksmith shop gave in and creaked as he paced the room. Though the location was perfect—for no one suspected the strong slaves venturing here for work—the constant fire had Jean sweating. He yearned for proper catches that would let him leave more of the heavy work to others. "What did Prudence bubble around this time?"

"He posted a public letter claiming to have heard a smuggler state the governor overstepped his powers."

Under them, a slave kindled the small furnace—the bigger one was in the adjoining house—and pumped air into the now crackling flames. Jean nodded with a mockingly serious expression, the taste of molten metal creeping onto his tongue as the smoke rose through the floorboards like ghosts rising from the dead. "Oh, even the patient Claiborne cannot ignore this." Jean snickered, fetched another sack and yanked it over his shoulder. Having grown up in Bordeaux, and so close to the Pyrenees Mountains—a lawless region that separated France from Spain, and which he often visited for much of his family lived there—he had never had the chance to feel himself part of either country or sympathy for its organizers, be it king or government. But Jean was also a sociable man who cared about people, business relationships and social standing, and he knew this was the point Mr. Clark was trying to touch. Jean smiled. "But for once, I fear Prudence is right."

Mr. Clark exhaled and strode forward, pushing away the smoke between them. "True or not, your disguise is crumbling."

Jean lifted the sack onto the rack and offered Mr. Clark a smug smile. But seeing Mr. Clark's tense expression, Jean's faded. He shrugged before picking up the next brown sack.

Heavy clinks from the blacksmith's hammering silenced Mr. Clark before he could speak, and the vibration of the hits thrummed through the wood. It ended with sizzling.

"Vincent Nolte complained that the French Creole planters make no secret of obtaining slaves at a hundred and fifty dollars on Barataria instead of the legal seven hundred here in the city."

Jean raised his brows, showing his open palms. "Cheap prices give us the support of the people."

"Mr. Nolte is an influential merchant, and we are compromising his business. Not to mention the scarcity of free money your no-check method is causing in town. The Governor claims it's driving a wedge between the French and Americans." Mr. Clark lowered his voice, and Jean heard tiny claws race over wood beyond him. "We are making allies and foes alike, Jean. And our friends may be *en masse*, but our enemies have power."

Jean puffed. "You fret too much. Don't forget I outwit their bureaucracy."

"My point, precisely." Mr. Clark hit one fist into the other. "We are not just taking their trade but parading the fact under their noses. We are provoking them."

"That's the merit of our business," Jean said, grinning widely.

"You are unbelievable, Laffite."

He gave Mr. Clark a lopsided smile, but, with no improvement in his companion's demeanor, sighed. "Fine, silence Prudence if you must, but do not hurt him."

CHAPTER 2

THE LADY IN RED

Jean had a weakness for observing people dance—a light-hearted expression of joy he yearned for at sea. The masked balls of New Orleans had none to compare, and so he often breathed against a humid disguise. He swirled the whiskey in his hand, enjoying the way it climbed up the sides of the glass like excited water in a tornado.

The music and dancing recessed and a horde of perfumed and masqueraded people trotted from the dance floor to the table with refreshments, shoes clonking on the wooden floor like hooves. The wide dresses caressed the ground, and their wearers' red cheeks, where visible, glistened with excitement.

Two men passed before Jean. One carried a walking stick—a cane with an adorned metal grip—and coat that reached his calves in the back, the other wore a hat, a glass of wine in his hand. Jean overheard the man with the cane say, "… disagree. The high ladies are infatuated by Laffite, monsieur Inspector."

Jean spilled whisky on his shoes. After jerking the drops

off, he followed the men, ensuring a tight fit of his mask. For learning opinions firsthand profited his business. Or at least that's what he told himself.

"You consider it too soon," the Inspector, wearing the tall hat with thick, waved rim, said as he settled on a chaise longue beside a table and lit a cigar. The spicy scent passed Jean like fog as the man smoked.

"Monsieur Inspector, let him make a mistake—in the public's eye, mind you—then strike."

Jean stood beside the men, who now glanced at him. He bowed at a passing woman and settled into the softness of an armchair facing away, clinking his glass on the wooden table beside it.

"I quite agree," the Inspector said. "As it stands, the people side with the smugglers rather than their own government. He tempts them with cheap goods, the scoundrel."

Jean scoffed. The word had a bitter aftertaste, and he shook his head, then gulped the whiskey, letting the aromatic sting of the spirit dissipate into the crevices of his mouth. He treated everyone with respect and spared not a penny for any captured person's safety and convenience. He never touched their belongings and paid their fare home. Jean was a gentleman.

"Meanwhile, we must extend the investigation."

"No doubt Claiborne will have to heed your word now, Monsieur Inspector."

"Quite so, 'Prudence' has made a point of it."

For the last time ... A smirk crossed Jean's lips as his gaze wandered over the library beside him. The small orchestra resumed with a slow waltz as a woman's gentle voice caught Jean's attention. "Would you spare a dance, Inspector Gilbert?"

Jean turned around to a delicate beige dress adorned with vibrant flowers, topped with a hat of the same fashion. She knew the Inspector well, or she wouldn't have recognized him by his posture alone.

"I am humbled by your kind gesture, Madame, but I am not in a condition to dance tonight."

Jean watched the woman pace into the throng with a sunken head and felt a pang in his heart.

The Inspector behind Jean whispered. "In fact, I am awaiting a darling with a red feathered mask."

"The Wolf?"

"I confess, she has me under her spell. I would not have moved our meeting here had it not been for her."

Jean let his finger glide over the cool cup as he let this information sicker in. Though his heart beat for privateering, he also had an influence on women. He considered wooing the woman in question to reveal information obtained from the Inspector. Or at least find amusement in his newfound Platonic duel with him.

"I doubt she is likewise inclined unless she is under the spell of fear, monsieur Inspector. Or the prospect of wealth should you succeed in your endeavor with the smugglers."

The Inspector laughed, and his voice was husky with cigar. "All clever women are under the spell of my prospects, sir." A sweet-musky fragrance passed Jean in a veil of smoke. "She's a stunning beauty."

"For a mulatto—"

"Tut."

The man with the walking stick cleared his throat. "I must ask, do you not find it suspicious she keeps company with so many officials?"

"I shall put an end to that. In fact, I am proposing she become my mistress tonight."

"That's rather ambitious."

"What woman could refuse a reliable income, her own home in the city, and me to keep company?"

The Inspector's companion lowered his tone and his walking stick fell to the floor with a clonk. "They don't call her Wolf for nothing. Do not make your association with her public, monsieur Inspector. Especially after the ... incident."

A welcome gust of wind brought in fresh air and scents of cut grass from the large windows, which flew open. Outside, the heavy gates creaked, and the whispering grew inaudible. Jean gave up on discovering more about the Wolf as he sighted a red feathered mask. He shot up, strode to the woman and offered a dance, his hand held out.

She curtsied. "I'm tired, sir. Apologies." Her voice was low but not masculine, and when she spun around, Jean held onto her wrist. It was a naked lie as she had an appointment with the Inspector.

"Mademoiselle Wolf."

The jerk of her head undid the woman's mask, which slipped, revealing all of her large hazel eyes striking Jean, above the full lips the color of her dress and mask. Jean's heart leaped. He understood how she could have the Inspector spellbound, even though Jean did not keep company with such women himself. The Inspector seemed confident enough in his own charms, but Jean doubted he flattered as many of the fair sex as he claimed. Certainly not a lady as fine as her.

"What do ye want, sir?" Her tone was demanding, and Jean realized she spoke no French, but a strange mixture of accents he couldn't pin out—there was a Creole influence, perhaps some Irish—and in stark contrast to her lady-like appearance.

The tinge of fear in her voice made him aware once again of the power of information applied with a hue of wit, and he offered his hand. "Fear not, I wish merely a waltz, mademoiselle." With that, he bowed, and she chuckled. Then he felt the warmth of her fingers on his palm.

"Do I know ye?" she said as they twirled a fast waltz under the tall, ornamented ceiling.

Wolf's muscles jumped beneath the silky corset—she was not like the fragile French women Jean mixed with. "Not yet, mademoiselle."

"Then how do ye know me name?" A glimmer of suspicion shone from her eyes, and her fingers trembled in his. Was she scared? She appeared young, perhaps eighteen, and struggling to disguise it. He adopted an impish smile, hoping to ease her discomfort.

"I've heard of it, mademoiselle."

Wolf let out a chuckle and her eyes softened, and with a tone rich in playful satisfaction, she said, "Oh oh! I didn't realize I was so popular."

As they passed the Inspector and his companion still sitting at the table, Jean gave the staring men a full grin. "All eyes are on you, mademoiselle."

Then her laugh turned serious, and he led her to the other end of the hall. He kissed her hand, leaving a sour taste of soap with a salty tang on his lips. "It was a pleasure, mademoiselle, and I hope we meet again."

Wolf curtsied and said, "Aye, so do I."

If Jean knew the power of knowledge, now was the moment to use it to woo her. In his experience, such mental features impressed women. Wolf's hand still in his, he moved closer and whispered. "At your rendezvous with Inspector Gilbert, please let him know Laffite sends his deepest regrets for having kept you away." He left her standing agape. Wolf grabbed his sleeve, and he twisted around to free his arm. "Mademoiselle, this isn't proper for a lady."

Mademoiselle dropped her mask again—so sharp was the jerk she pulled Jean towards her with—and she whispered in a low pitch. "Take it as proof I long not to be a lady, but a pirate. Assume me in your company."

If Jean had expected his charms to take effect, he had not predicted this response. All he wanted was to woo her for information, and the surprise showed in his voice. "A woman assist me, mademoiselle? My men are not suitable society for a fine lady."

"Then we are clear on one thing—that I will not assist but work beside ye as an equal."

Now it was Jean's turn to gape. "You are quite unordinary, mademoiselle." Her eyes glowed amber in the candle-light, reminiscent of a wolf's. "Why a pirate?"

"I want to kill the Inspector."

Jean stepped back, his finger on his lips to signal silence. Her expression remained serious, and he moved close again. "Whatever for?"

"He killed me mother."

"*Mon Dieu* ..." He gazed over her wide frock and the caramel cleavage, propping over her corset, and swallowed. "Then you require an assassin, for I am no murderer—I rather consider myself to be a gentleman." He made obeisance, and being so close, his hair skimmed her shoulder.

Wolf observed his display with a lopsided smile. "Gentleman pirate, I know. Ye can help me get back at him before I kill him."

"I do not wish to harm anyone, mademoiselle." Jean grimaced. "You won't tally."

Wolf stepped closer and peered at Jean with curled lips.

"I can deliver him wrong information and tell ye what he is plotting."

Jean puffed, eyes wide. "So that's your spell—bribery." His eyebrows lingered on his forehead.

"Aye, I'm rather talented at it."

Inhaling the stuffy, sweet air, Jean rubbed his chin. "How shall I find you?"

"Me name is Cosma Wolfe, ye may meet me at the Moulin Rouge on Gallatin Street if ye dare. I'll be expecting yer call."

Jean laughed, then caught the eye of a gentleman and covered his lips to hush himself. He whispered, "You're an adventuress?" The Gallatin Street was by far the most dangerous place he knew and where rumors even told of men butchered on the streets by angry prostitutes. That's why she chose a masked ball for a meeting place—a public place where she would be safe and yet disguised. "Why does this not surprise me?"

Cosma leaned forward, her warm breath brushing against his ear. "Perhaps ye have an adventurous mind, sir." Then she curtsied and pushed into the brood, and Jean's gaze followed her until she disappeared in it.

CHAPTER 3
A COLD FRIEND

ississippi, October 1813

The pirogue Jean sat in was so close to the water he could hear it splash against the sides as it glided through the night. He reached out and let the cool and soft liquid brush along his hand, then let the drops that trembled at his fingertips drip into the Mississippi. He enjoyed this intimacy with the river, and it reminded him of his childhood where he and his brother Pierre spent days building boats and racing on the Garonne river near Bordeaux, sometimes even on the Bay of Biscay.

But civilization was taking its toll on the Mississippi. Upriver butcher shops and factories used the giant liquid snake, esteemed by the natives that still lived along it, as a waste system. With the modern steamboat *New Orleans* occasionally passing up and down, this pollution was already increasing. Jean didn't like it one bit—neither for the odor it caused nor the danger it posed to his operation.

And yet his business at sea bore risks, too. The schooners he used on the Gulf towered above the salty mass he so loved, and more than once, his drinking water fouled. He remembered times when he sailed from Bordeaux and had to resort to alcohol for fear of dying of thirst, falling full-fledged into the dangers of the mighty blue. Here on the Mississippi he could cook water to make it drinkable, and this comforted him.

A sound in the bushes at the shore startled Jean. He froze, trying to catch a distinctive clink of metal that would betray human presence. A hand raised in one boat ahead, their code for attention. The others had noticed it, too. The boats continued their pace, and the men froze, eyes and ears facing the moonlit riverbank.

You better not be out here, Inspector. Since Gilbert's seizure on the Lafourche ten days ago, the Inspector had caused Jean a headache. Just the previous evening, Gilbert had captured nine bales of fabric. Though this wasn't a minor loss, the significant casualty was that of their hiding place along the river. If Gilbert discovered more of them, Jean's business was in jeopardy. A year ago, Jean would have surrendered if Gilbert had attacked him. But not now. Now he would fight back.

The boats pressed ahead, gurgling as their fronts diverged the water. They were nearing the jutting spit of land from which one planter-spy had already reported Jean's smuggling to the authorities. It would be difficult returning now, and the next hiding place was miles away.

And then there it was. The distinctive metallic click of a musket latch. Jean sensed the eyes of his men on him. He shut his and exhaled, and when screams came from the attackers at the first boat, lifted his hand with spread out fingers—their signal to disperse and land any goods they could take along.

He navigated the remaining boats across the current and past the attackers. Under the rising moon, he spotted four men in a small boat leaping onto the first of his caravan. Their high-pitched screaming told Jean they weren't confident about their endeavor—scanty volunteers Gilbert recruited with the prospect of a share in the reward. They could not catch more boats, and Jean would get to safety. As they drifted past the yelling men, Jean glimpsed Gilbert's figure.

"That's enough, Gilbert," Jean whispered. Then Jean and the boats not seized took up speed and landed the freight on the shore opposite the attack. "Hide the goods under brush and wood," Jean said as he climbed off, jaw clenching. His shoes squelched in the mud and he had to use all his force to heave the boat towards the dry. He rubbed his sleeve across his forehead and pulled the wood plank out as far as he could. Its end drowned in the sludge.

He shrugged, then held out his hand to help the others carrying the goods walk across it without falling.

Cosma materialized beside him, wearing her corset dress that only reached her knees. "I will get him back for this."

Jean puffed. "Please stay in the boat, mademoiselle."

Cosma nodded but waded to another boat and carried goods away. He knew it would be of no avail to stop her, so he watched the muscled outline of her calves disappear in the thicket, then grabbed merchandise himself and followed.

WHEN THEY GATHERED at the waterfront again, Jean beckoned everyone. "We'll take cover at the bank opposite." It was a tactic Jean had gained with his smuggling experience—if

Gilbert discovered the loot, he wouldn't search for the men, and if Gilbert discovered the men, they couldn't be considered smugglers with no loot on them. The men's sweaty faces relaxed, and soon their boats glided over the serene waters. The sky was turning orange in the distance and the trees swayed with a slight breeze. Jean patted the smooth edge of the boat with his eyebrows knotted. "You will regret this, Gilbert."

The night was silent except for the crickets and occasional plop in the wet. They waded through the grass at the riverbank, the cool and sharp blades brushing their calves, and, bearing the boats on their shoulders, they formed a train. Jean was under the front boat, leading his men into the forest. Earth stuck to their wet feet and made trickling noises as they traipsed. A muffled thump at the front, accompanied by pain where a cross beam dug into his shoulder, startled him. The four men under his boat suppressed laughter before the boat following thumped into them. Jean had bumped into a tree.

"*Desolé*,"—sorry—Germain said behind him. The main reason Jean took Germain—the man constantly grinning—along was for his humor.

Jean grunted and stepped around the tree, only to stumble on one of its roots sticking out of the soil. Catching himself before tearing the boat and the four other men carrying it to the ground, Jean said, "today is not my day." The men under his boat broke out in laughter. The ones further behind shooed them and whispered, "*fils de taupe*," —son of a mole—and other creative insults in French.

They set up camp near a tree enclosed with bushes. "I'll take the first guard shift," Jean said and planted himself on a rock, leaning against the tree.

As it drizzled, the others placed the branches and rocks

they could find under one side of the boats to create tilted roofs and laid under them.

Jean enjoyed observing the nocturnal harmony fade. The stringed insects and birds announced sunrise as the fragrance of the opening flower buds and the calm power of the morning sun spread over the forest. Birds leaped to the ground, picked out delicacies and shot back into the branches, and a few moths fluttered through the disappearing mist in search of darkness. Except now it was accompanied by snoring.

Cosma appeared playing with a twig and slumped beside him. He eyed the stretched-out legs caked with drying mud. Occasional drops from above darkened the clay where they fell on it. "Were you aware of Gilbert's presence?" he said.

"No." Cosma twisted the green branch and pulled off its leaves, dispersing them beside her.

"Because it seemed perfect for a confrontation ..."

She broke the twig and flicked it away. "No, Fita. I'll kill him on me own."

Jean felt the rage vibrate within her, and it made his own stronger. Once again, Gilbert had cut him off right before success. *"L'enculleur de mouche,"*—fly fucker—Jean whispered, knowing Cosma understood little French.

Jean's rival with the authorities went back to his childhood. The Bourbon kings of France ruined his father's business with taxation and church levies, not to mention the turmoils of the French Revolution that followed. When the young and enthusiastic captain Napoleon Bonaparte stepped into the political battlefield, Jean had had enough and sailed to what he imagined a better life.

"Aye. The trade is catching up with ye." Cosma eyed him with a lopsided smile.

Jean adjusted his shirt. "What trade? Piracy?"

"Aye. Ye're a pirate proper now, Fita."

"I prefer to be a gentleman, foremost."

Cosma rolled her eyes. "There we go again …"

Jean leaned his head back on the trunk of the tree and lost his gaze in the foliage above. The little drops falling onto the leaves and boats created a soothing rhythm, accompanied by the distant gurgling of the Mississippi and the forest inhabitants waking.

Cosma's voice was dry, like the clay on her feet. "I practice shooting now."

"Indeed?" Jean shot her a glance. "I'd have expected your weapon of choice to be a sword, given your temper, but—"

"I have no temper."

"*Non*, forgive me, mademoiselle." Something cool grazed the nape of his neck, raising his hairs. He turned and gasped. "A Queen Anne. The epitome of style for a lady." He took the elegant and generously decorated pistol and inspected it. "Truly the perfect weapon for a woman. But you'd have to get rather close to your victim." Jean held the pistol out and Cosma snatched it.

"Then it's fortunate I do."

Jean nodded. "Where do you keep it? You don't carry a bag or coat, and no muffles, either."

Cosma grinned and lifted her skirt.

"Mademoiselle!"

She laughed and tucked the pistol into the ribbon around her thigh. "Any man getting too close will encounter me cold friend first."

Jean puffed. "Or you could slick up a respectable dress."

"And get stuck on every twig I pass, looking like a

shaggy street dog by evening?" Cosma shook her head. "No, thank ye. Besides, I like me style."

"Ah ..." Jean yawned and leaned his head on the tree. His eyes watered from exhaustion, and a tear crawled down each side of his face.

CHAPTER 4

PLANS BY THE RIVER

Jean Laffite woke to Germain and a few others gathered before him, dividing the few provisions they had brought for the passage. "What's the plan, Captain?" Germain said.

Jean yawned and stretched, then stood up, back cracking. "Sleep."

"*Non*, seriously."

Jean sauntered to the nearest boat. Gilbert would look for him, so hiding was the best option for now. It was drizzling again, and the cool drops tickled as they trickled through his hair. "Pierre will have news and send help. Meanwhile, one of you spy on the river. If any allies pass, bring them here." Then he squatted to look beneath the boat, a whiff of morning breath from the man snoring under it welcoming him.

"So your plan is to wait for your brother?" said Germain.

"You're wanted for smuggling, Captain, I wouldn't stay out here," said Fulbert—the shy but quick-thinking young Frenchman.

Jean shot his companions a puzzled gaze. "They'll patrol the water."

Fulbert shrugged, his palms facing forward. "What about the reward for your apprehension? If anyone passes here—"

"They won't patrol the bush," Jean said, then slipped under the boat and laid down beside a snoring comrade.

"I agree with Fita," Jean heard Germain say. "We're so close to Mayronne's, and he'll come looking once he gets word. He's eager to get the goods."

Jean closed his eyes and let his back, aching from having leaned on the rough bark for hours, relax.

"Isn't the reward for apprehension a rumor?" said Bertrand, whom Jean took along for his physical strength—and who was eager to display it at all times.

Alexandre's quaky voice said, "No one even knows which Laffite it's for."

Germain's tone was soft with concern. "Still, if someone tries their luck, the authorities will have Fita for smuggling."

Jean melted into slumber.

Jean woke to drumming on the upside-down boat, shoving at his legs and the fragrance of rain touching earth.

"The goods," Fulbert cried.

They hoisted the boats and stood up—for the rain was so heavy it formed puddles that ran under the protection.

Jean rose, rubbing his face. "Whether they got wet cannot be helped." He yawned. "We'll wait until it stops and then row across."

Soon after, they found Germain shivering at his post on the river bank. When the rain ceased, they crossed.

"*Caca boudin!*"—poop sausage—Germain said, unraveling the soaked and muddy linen.

Cosma appeared with a dripping box of cigars. "*Mes cuilles sur ton front,*"—my balls on your nose—she said stomping towards the others. The men glanced at each other, some shocked, others muffling their laughter. "See," Cosma said to Jean, "I tally just fine."

Jean scratched his nose, holding back laughter. "There's a missing technicality ..."

"Oh—oh, come now boys," Cosma said, grinning. "Ye say it all the time." Then she headed to the river bank, leaving puzzled faces.

Germain cleared his throat and said, "mademoiselle, where are you going?"

"The cigars won't dry in the shade, Germain. Unless ye want to sell cigars that have fashioned their own forest."

Germain glanced at Jean's fingers playing with the roughness of the bark of the tree he leaned on. "*Oui,*" said Jean. "She's right. We'll set up two guards, one at each end, and the remaining will stay at the shore ready to pack up the wares should the guards send a signal."

They spent the rest of the day spreading out the goods on the bank and turning them every few hours to dry all sides—all the while fearing being discovered. They ate little and drank the muddy river water, the tiny particles grinding between their teeth. On the second day, Jean paced the bank, his feet squelching in the mud near the water. He stopped and turned to the others. "This is ridiculous. I'm walking downriver to inform Mayronne."

"I'll come with ye," Cosma said, shooting up and dusting her skirt.

Germain squelched beside Jean. "*Moi aussi,*"—me too.

The other men nodded and returned to staring over the river.

Cosma tucked her arm under Jean's, and the three walked along the bank. He inhaled the algae scent rising from the sluicing water, and its powerful aroma filled his senses. The crickets had the courtesy to stop screeching as they passed, and a bird near them fled and flapped across the river, settling on a tree hanging over the water at the other shore.

"When will we return to Barataria?" Cosma smiled.

Jean let out a laugh. "Soon enough, mademoiselle."

Cosma looked pensively at the water as a fish jumped and landed back in the river with a splash. "I miss the ocean."

Germain took her other arm. "Barataria Bay is hardly an ocean, mademoiselle."

She shot him a darting glance. "I know. But I can't remember much from me journey here, I was so young." She turned to Jean. "What's it like out there as a pirate?"

"Boring," Germain said.

Cosma raised her sleek brows. "I've never met a bored pirate."

"Because you have met none at sea," Jean said, remembering months on end not able to decide which was worse —the boredom or the lack of food and water.

A smile snuck onto Cosma's lips. "Have ye ever visited other islands?"

"Of course," Germain said.

Cosma gasped and spun back to Jean. "Which ones?"

"Why are you asking?" Jean said and winked at Germain. "Do you suppose I have a treasure buried somewhere?"

Germain snickered and raised his thick brows at Cosma.

Cosma said, "I may need me own island one day."

Germain stumbled over a decaying branch, catching himself with a smirk.

"You are ambitious, mademoiselle," said Jean.

"Oh, ye'll see, Fita. Better turn in me good graces now, for ye'll fear me when I strike."

"What strikes me is your confidence, mademoiselle," Jean said.

Her eyes slanted as her index finger flew to her mouth. Jean halted hearing hooves. A sharp tingling ran through his veins, and the tiny hairs on his limbs rose and pressed against his clothing. Someone was out there.

"Laffite," a man called out from afar. Could this be word from Pierre?

"Do you recognize the voice?" Germain whispered as he grabbed Jean's arm.

Jean gazed over the rotten deadfall and leaves, eyebrows furrowed. "*Non.*"

A dragonfly zoomed past them and disappeared into the tall grass by the river.

Cosma exhaled and swung her hand as if brushing aside any uncertainty. "It's Mayronne's messenger."

"It could be a trap." Jean wrinkled his nose at a whinny from the same direction.

The hooves became louder. "Jean Laffite, a letter from Dumon."

"Dumon!" Germain said and stepped backwards.

"I am here," shouted Jean.

As the horse drew closer, Jean shifted, gripping his musket. When he halted his horse, the bony horseman handed Jean a note and waited for him to read it. Jean exhaled and opened the seal, and his face flushed when he reached the end. He nodded at the horseman, who trotted off.

Germain peered over the letter, but Jean knew it was for Cosma's sake, for Germain couldn't read. "Is Pierre coming?"

"Better yet." Jean locked eyes with Germain. "Gilbert is."

Cosma gasped. "What do ye mean?"

"He's transporting the confiscated merchandise down the river to New Orleans this evening." Jean let a boyish smile sneak onto his lips. "I warned Gilbert I would get my goods back, didn't I?"

Cosma laughed, and squinting, flapped a cocky finger at him. "Say one more time ye're a gentleman, Fita."

Then Jean offered Cosma his arm, and Germain joined them with a grin.

CHAPTER 5

QUEEN ANNE

The smugglers cheered at the news that restored their good spirits. More than once, Gilbert had taken a hard week's work from them—now was their chance to return the favor.

Jean raised his voice over their mumbling and chuckles. "There won't be many men aboard. We only need fear Gilbert, for he'll fall to passion when he finds out what circumstance has struck him."

"I'll handle him." Cosma's husky voice had an alluring sternness that drowned in the ramble.

Jean shook his head. "*Non*, mademoiselle, this mission is far too dangerous."

Cosma slipped her hand between her thighs, at which the smugglers fell silent, then presented her Queen Anne. "I'll take the risk."

The group nodded, some chuckled and mumbled, and Jean's incredulous stare locked on Cosma's hazel eyes as the men dispersed to hide the goods once again in the forest.

When Jean's men laid in hiding with bellies on the soil and heads propped with their elbows, Jean positioned himself beside Cosma. As the night grew thick, his foot twitched and his fingers trembled on the cold iron of his musket. Glancing over at Cosma, he said, "You undermine me in front of my lot. You are playing a game not yours to play."

Cosma raised her slender brows in his direction. Was there a smirk on her lips? "The situation has changed," she said, "so must our tactics."

Jean puffed. "*Oui*, but I will not grant you orders, and neither position you between fires, mademoiselle."

"I can take care of meself," Cosma said, peering over the sluicing water.

Jean's breath rustled the leaves before him, as if they escaped the anger vibrating within him. "What will people think of me?"

Cosma offered him a bemused gaze, cocking her head. "That ye're a pirate proper, aye?"

Jean threw his musket on the ground before him and sat up. "I cannot allow it."

Cosma turned to her side, her Queen Anne loose in her hand, and chuckled. "I don't need yer permission."

"If you want to be on your own hook," Jean said and pinched his lips.

"Ye cannot avoid violence any longer, Fita." Cosma sat up, the moon's light reflecting in her amber eyes, once again reminiscent of a wolf. "What difference does it make if I'm there?"

"You're a woman."

Cosma laughed and ignored Jean's beckoning her silence. "Ye expect when Gilbert is dead, ye'll be rid of me, aye?"

He glanced at the outlines of the musket in the sand, his face hot. "*Non*, mademoiselle. You are challenging and refreshing company." He picked up the weapon, put it on his lap, and sighed. "But I cannot promise Gilbert will survive the night, and as you mentioned yourself, his demise was your reason for joining my lot."

"Oh, oh." Cosma's full lips spread in a wide beam. "Ye have me all wrong, Fita."

Jean rubbed the earth from his elbows, which trickled onto the withered leaves. "What do you mean?"

Cosma let out a deep chuckle that gurgled in her throat like the river they sat by. "I'm a pirate, too."

"*Mon Dieu*." Jean held the back of his hand at his forehead and took on a dramatic tone. "The seven seas quiver."

"Ye mock me now, Fita." She gave him a lopsided smile.

Jean cleared his throat. "If you try to kill Gilbert in anything other than self-defense, you will be a lonely pirate from tomorrow, mademoiselle."

Cosma's voice picked up an alluring richness. "Gilbert is not the only official I have wrapped around me finger." She twirled the Queen Anne around her index like a lasso. "I can pull more strings than ye might suspect."

Jean cocked his head. "Like who?"

"I won't tell ye." Was that a sneer? She leaned forward and whispered, her warm breath brushing up against his face. "If ye turn against me, ye'll see yer trade sink bottom faster than ye can imagine."

Jean's fingers stung from tightening his grip on the musket. He turned away. "You'll not go alone," he said, staring into the black void beyond the river.

Cosma shrugged. "I have me Queen Anne."

"*Non*," said Jean. "A man shall accompany you."

"If that rests yer soul, Fita." She turned onto her stomach again and stared at the water.

• • •

THEY SPENT the night waiting for a boat that did not pass. When sunrise tickled the fog above the river, the men gathered at the shore.

"Maybe something held him back," said Germain, yawning and slumped on a smooth rock.

Jean looked into the foggy distance over the Mississippi. "We need information. We must know when he is coming."

"Monsieur Gaudins has land on the west bank," Fulbert said, playing with the hem of his shirt. "We could walk there."

Some men nodded, others studied Jean.

Bertrand stood beside Cosma with a wide stance, and arms folded. "That's hardly a few miles upstream of New Orleans," he said.

Jean sighed. "We'll risk it. Besides, we're all hungry." He beckoned Germain. "You and I shall go ahead. The rest follow with the merchandise."

As the others returned to their hiding place, Cosma strolled up beside Jean.

"*Mais*, you cannot come with us, mademoiselle."

"Why not?" Her expression was serious, but a smirk tickled the edge of her lips.

Jean swayed his head, and Germain adopted a gentle tone. "People will assume he takes his concubines on his missions."

"So?" Cosma peered at him, tucking her arm under his.

Jean paused, removed her hand, and bore it between his. "*Non*, I won't have it."

Cosma chuckled. "That people suppose I'm yer adventuress or that ye take 'em to business?"

"Both."

"I'll make certain they learn neither is true." Cosma

winked at him, and his face burned with heat. *Undermine him again?*

His tone was harsh. "You'll do nothing of the kind, mademoiselle."

Cosma slipped her arm under Germain's, who accepted with a wavering smile.

"Come now, Fita," she said in a tone vibrant with mockery. "Ye needn't worry."

Heart pounding, he marched ahead. "I should never have accepted you coming on this expedition."

CHAPTER 6

GUESTS FOR MONSIEUR GAUDINS

"I wish to see monsieur Gaudins," Jean said to the servant coming down the stairs to receive the visitors.

"He is expecting you, sir. Please follow me."

The trio glanced at each other, their rugged clothes hanging limp. Then they followed the elegant man into the house and to the dining hall. As they neared it, Jean's stomach growled at the fragrance of food. There stood arranged a table with fresh bread, butter, plates and glasses. Then he noticed the people sitting around it.

"Mayronne," Jean said as he strode to shake his hand. "What a surprise. I'm glad you're here. We're in a pickle of the finest."

Mayronne's voice had a serious tone. "So I heard. I've brought Mr. Whiteman for aid." Mayronne stepped backwards to reveal the man, who wiped his lips with a serviette, dropped it beside his plate and rose. Jean recognized the tall man of upright posture—an excellent gunman, as Jean recalled. So everyone knew violence was no longer an option.

In by the door sauntered monsieur Gaudins with a bottle of wine. "Alas, we thought you'd never come, Captain." Monsieur Gaudins stopped mid-stride as he set eyes on Cosma.

"I've brought Germain and mademoiselle Wolfe," said Jean.

Germain shook hands with the company, and Cosma curtsied, seizing the hem of her skirt. Jean turned to Mayronne and said, "What is your word on the whereabouts of inspector Gilbert, gentlemen?"

"He should pass any day now, and fortunately," monsieur Gaudins walked to the window, the wooden floorboards creaking beneath his weight, and tugged aside the curtain. "We have a view of the river."

"Excellent." Jean clapped. "My men will be here within the next hours."

"Meanwhile," said Mr. Whiteman, "We shall get you strong and confident with food and wine."

Monsieur Gaudins beckoned the party to sit, poured wine into the glasses and distributed them.

"And what business does the misses have in this?" Mr. Whiteman said as Cosma settled opposite him.

Jean's face flushed as he shot Cosma a darting gaze.

Her lips curled. "I'm here on my personal insistence. Inspector Gilbert owes me a considerable sum and refuses to pay. But my intention is purely demonstrational, I assure you."

Jean glanced at Germain to see if Cosma's excellent pronunciation and her lady-like manner surprised Germain, too, then nodded at monsieur Gaudins's raised brows. Cosma hadn't put on an act such as this even when Jean had met her at the ball in New Orleans where she certainly looked the part a lady. But sitting there with the napkin spread on her stained dress, her arms, face and low cleavage sandy and her butter knife swinging with elegance, she gave an obscure but even better impression of a lady.

But, too hungry to give the matter much more thought, Jean ate several slices, letting the soft, aromatic bread and fresh butter melt on his tongue. He leaned back, and the thin wood of the chair gave in creaking. With a pang, Jean realized the caked mud on his, Cosma's and Germain's feet had left trails of dirt on the floor, reminding him of his difficult situation.

Jean sighed, and Mayronne turned to him, and said, "what merchandise did Gilbert capture?"

Jean's knuckles turned white as he gripped the edge of the table. "Only one boat."

"Remaining are four pounds of cloves," Germain said, and wiped his mouth. "Seven pounds of raisins, hundred-twenty-five candles—"

"Two bars of iron," Cosma said. "Fifteen silk stockings, a hundred and forty-nine cigars ..."

Jean straightened. "And twenty-three gallons of brandy."

"Twenty-two," Germain said with a lopsided smile.

"We will raid this and more when he passes." Mr. Whiteman drank his wine in one go.

Germain nodded. "I suspect he has been accumulating goods over the last week at least, or we would have seen him pass."

Mayronne cleared his throat. "In that case, I shall delay purchase until all goods are present, Captain."

Jean knew Mayronne did not want to risk settling for wares and seeing them confiscated, should his mission fail.

But he didn't care—Gilbert would not escape. "Sir, you have yourself a deal."

When the men retired, Germain sat by the window. Jean excused himself, followed Cosma to her guest room, and closed the door. He drove the metal bar into its latch, forcing the door up by its handle to make the screeching less loud. Then he eyed Cosma, yawning. "Your motive is demonstrational?"

She sat on a mattress on the floor and shrugged, her weary eyes peering up at him. "I want him to see me."

"Why?" He kept his wide stance and crossed arms. It was one time too many. She had fabricated plans without informing him and exposed them to his men, leaving Jean as astonished as everyone else. Not merely because, as a member of the fair sex, she was not supposed to concern herself with the plans of his men, but because she accomplished said plans. It felt as if she was taking his control, and he didn't appreciate it one bit.

Cosma glanced out the narrow window, drew the Queen Anne from her thigh and stuck it under the pillow. "I want him to believe I was behind this."

"You could tell him." He moved closer, and the algae odor of river lingering on the linen of the bed increased.

Peering up, she said, "it's not the same."

"I understand." Jean sat beside her and sank into the softness of the cotton-stuffed mattress. "But it's dangerous."

Cosma laid on the cushion and slanted her eyes. "It's amusing how ye care for me safety, yet will not share a bed with me."

Fingers tingling, he rubbed them against his knees. "You are a woman, hence I must ensure your safety."

"I understand why, Fita. I've met plenty like ye. But it changed not one."

"What?"

Cosma's rich tone turned serious and her hazel eyes stung him as if they stared into his soul. "Ye trade slaves, Fita. So ye think ye shouldn't get familiar with anyone with some color. Ye worry it'll change ye mind about them. Ye're scared ye'll realize ye're not the gentleman ye claim."

"This is far beside the point, mademoiselle." He wiped his palms on the outside of his thighs.

Cosma sat up, her face so close to his he could almost taste the butter from lunch as she spoke. "Everyone has a dark side, Jean. Embrace it."

"With all due respect, mademoiselle," he said, his voice becoming husky. "Knowledge and intimacy are weapons not entrustable to you." He shook his head. "I shall not reveal more than you have already seen."

Cosma lay on the cushion again, eyes gleaming. "Time will tell."

"*Non*, I am telling you." He exhaled. "Besides, if you're not planning to kill Gilbert now, how will you get close enough to him to shoot your Queen Anne without risking apprehension?"

Cosma's voice was low and steady, as was her eye contact. "The pistol is only for self-protection. Me plans with Gilbert are far from over."

"And how are you going to accomplish your objectives from afar?" The scent of stale air made its way onto his tongue, and he closed his mouth.

Cosma's eyebrows furrowed. "Ye underestimate me, Fita."

"I suppose I do," said Jean with a cocked head.

The wood creaked with a gust of wind, and it hissed

through holes at the window. Cosma's face melted into a smile, accompanied by a quirk in the brow. "Not only do I know his secrets—I am learned in voodoo."

"*Mon Dieu.*" Jean grabbed his chest. "You'll poke him to death with your dolls."

There was a sudden tension in Cosma's face, and her tone took on a challenging note as the wind's hissing subsided into a howl and receded. "Ye understand not what ye speak of, Fita."

At this, Jean's chest ached. "Very well," he said and folded his hands in his lap, staring at them. The Mississippi's distant sloshing now pressed on his ears like a colossal snake, unyielding on its way to the Gulf of Mexico. He had not meant to hurt her feelings. "Where do you learn such things?"

"Marguerite D'Arcantrel."

Jean straightened out the coarse cloth of his breeches. "Never heard of her."

Eyes relaxing, Cosma said, "Ye may be acquainted with Charles Laveau—they have an illegitimate daughter together."

"So that was your recent business," Jean said, a smile returning.

"Aye."

He kissed the back of her hand, warm beneath his lips. "I apologize. I do not have a secret to share." Then he stood up and opened the door.

Cosma yawned and winked. "Don't trouble yerself. I know ye inside out."

CHAPTER 7
A FEATHERED ASSOCIATE

Jean woke to the sound of splashing water, shot up and stared out the window to see Gaudins and a slave running to the river, shouting. Had they spotted Gilbert? He couldn't see the river from this room, what with all the bushes in between. He imagined Gilbert's grinning face on the river as Jean slept, dreaming of the loot as it passed under his nose. Grunting, he slid his hand under the pillow to find but soft linen. Where had he left his musket?

As he paced through the hallway, he saw Whiteman pouring a cup of wine. "Where are the weapons?" Jean rubbed his eyes, the grit from sleep poking the inside corners.

Whiteman looked up and shook his head. "It's a crocodile, got one of his sheep. I advised him not to let them past the levee, but you know monsieur Gaudins."

Jean exhaled and slumped into a chair. "What is taking Gilbert so long?"

Whiteman handed him a cup, eying him. "He'll show up."

Jean let the fruity wine wake his senses. The cup thumped onto the wooden table and he grabbed an apple and bit into its crunch and rich-flavored juice.

"Captain," Whiteman said, "if I may be blunt, the presence of your woman affiliate is rather unsettling."

"I am well aware." He swallowed. "Yet she does not listen."

Whiteman cut an apple in half with a butter knife. "Is her endeavor truly for money? She appears ..." He placed the knife on the ceramic plate with a soft clink. "Passionate."

"I cannot say." Jean sat upright. "But one thing is certain, I will not allow her to accompany us again."

Whiteman gave him a curt nod. "A wise decision."

"For now," Jean said, pouring another cup of wine and swirling the sweet aroma under his nose. "Will you ensure her safety?"

"Oh ..." Whiteman focused on his plate as a pink color crept over his cheeks.

"I am asking as one gentleman to another."

"I see."

"But I warn you," Jean said, leaning forward and lowering his voice, "Stay a gentleman and say nothing of consequence." He shot a glance at the door. "Trust me, she will use it against you."

Whiteman's brows shot up, and a smile forced onto his lips. Now realizing he had given Whiteman the impression he had passed trade secrets to a woman—or worse, indulged in behavior not suitable for a gentleman—he said, "I haven't spoken a word, and she even uses that against me."

Whiteman burst into a laugh. "They're a passionate folk."

．　．　．

LATER IN THE AFTERNOON, Jean's men arrived with the cargoes, and the servants helped to clean them and spread them for drying. Evening drew near and passed.

After another rest, Jean took guard in the early morning hours. As the sun rose, it glistened pink in the pearls of dew that adorned the harp-shaped spider webs near the sodden shore. The river gurgled where its shallow waters passed between rocks. As he held the hard iron of his musket firm in one hand, Jean squelched through the mud and washed his face with water. Then he cupped his hand and drank a few milky sips.

There it was. A boat tiny in the distance, crawling upriver. Alas, Jean would get his revenge. Heart racing, he rushed back to the house, the cool morning air beating his face. He found the men asleep in the common room and woke grunting Whiteman, whom he instructed to wake the others. Then he raced back to the river to see a keelboat pass, cordelled by two slaves on the levee. To get the goods back from Gilbert now was an exquisite chance of revenge, and one that wouldn't present itself often.

There were three men on top of the cabin of the boat. He squinted—none of them was Gilbert. Jean's arms tightened with goosebumps from a cool breeze brushing its tiny hairs—Cosma rushed past him. She was interfering again. How could she? He reached for her shoulder, but she slipped away, running to the slaves passing on the levee. Their gasps sent adrenaline through Jean's veins, sharp and pounding. He needed reinforcements to attack. Now Cosma had revealed their presence. Teeth grinding, he followed, but stayed where he would not be seen.

Cosma screamed as if the river devoured her. Had she jumped into the current? He grunted and raced down the slope to see her gasping amidst the splashes, but as the two slaves jumped into the water after her, he stayed behind a bush and watched the keelboat slow and drift. Better to remain out of Gilbert's view. Perhaps Jean could still manage a surprise attack—if only Whiteman would show up. The men on top of the cabin took up the poles and pushed along the river bottom to propel forward. They were in a hurry.

Cosma's was an old trick—a lady in distress to distract, followed by an attack while the unsuspecting men let their guard down—except that Jean had had other plans, knowing Gilbert was no merchant but a trained inspector and would not fall for it.

Whiteman, Scott, and a mulatto came up beside Jean, carrying a pirogue on their backs. There was no time to waste, no resources to spare. "Follow the keelboat, fire in case of being fired at," Jean whispered, digging his fingers into Whiteman's lower arm. "Demand they surrender or I will fire from ashore. Do not let Gilbert escape." Whiteman nodded and beckoned the two men, then raced into the water and after the boat.

Once the keelboat was out of sight, Jean stepped to the levee where the two slaves were emerging from the water carrying Cosma. They put her down before Jean, and she grabbed onto his shoulder, unable to stand.

"I can't move my leg."

He reached around her waist and took her up, the cool river seeping through to his skin.

The slaves gestured towards the keelboat. "Must return to Master."

It was better they didn't—the less support Gilbert would have, the easier the attack would be. Jean smiled and beckoned them to follow him instead. "Your Master is coming here."

Their eyes grew damp with terror, and they looked at each other, back at Jean, and then darted toward the boat, mud flying behind them. Jean pinched his lips together and moved toward the house. "What happened?"

"I slipped on a rock." Cosma's voice was rough from her screams.

His breathing was heavy, and he cast a yearning glance at the receding plopping sound from the escaping slaves. Cosma was a member of the fairer sex, but not a frail one. "What were you thinking?"

"I wanted to swim to the boat." Cosma shrugged, and his arms trembled with the weight, driving his heels into the soft soil.

"Without knowing how to swim?" He adjusted his arms to prevent her from slipping. "You could have drowned, or a crocodile could have caught you."

"Gilbert was escaping."

How had he ever agreed to her coming along? She had no knowledge of the rivers or the unwritten laws of smuggling and was driven by a thoughtless confidence. He stopped and put her good foot on the ground, then stretched to look over the river. The pirogue was disappearing on the river's horizon. "If you would stop hankering and listen—"

"Let me sit on your back."

Jean gaped. "As on a mule?"

Cosma laughed, then the warmth of her body slung around Jean, as did the fishy river odor. Jean put one hasty step before another, and, leaning forward, he could smell the familiar whiff of stress-sweat emanating from his body. His mind conjured a number of creative swear words. Near the house, Gaudins appeared with two mulatto associates, and Jean put down Cosma.

A shout from far up the river sent a chill across his body and he un-hung the musket from his shoulder. It wasn't a light firearm, weighing twelve pounds, but with the recently developed percussion lock, it was reliable—which is why it was indispensable for Jean's expeditions both on the Mississippi and Barataria. It was—like Jean—tall and slender, elegant and yet simple, far-reaching and precise, and requiring particular attention to cleanliness.

Gaudins stepped beside Cosma and gestured Jean and the two men to run after the boat.

Cosma's voice carried down from the house. "Go get him, pirate."

Panting, Jean found the keelboat cornered at the shore, the pirogue empty behind it. They had already embarked. Gunshots fired. He felt the thrill of adventure hot on his skin. Now he was in his element. Fingers tight around his musket, he leaped onto the keelboat. Another musket fired into the cabin—with a muffled strike and flash—and he reached the view of its entrance, where Whiteman peered into it. His throat too dry from running, Jean's call to Whiteman went unheard. Whom had he fired at?

Whiteman stood at the door, bracing his musket with a wide stance. "Give up Mr. Laffite's goods."

Jean recognized Gilbert's voice—tainted with anger and fear. "You fool. They were never his."

As he drew up next to Whiteman at the cabin, Jean spotted Gilbert's eyes, which turned feverish when they set on him.

Jean didn't need to say a word—his presence told everything. It proved his warnings to Gilbert were genuine threats. And to think Cosma nearly cost him this moment.

He inhaled the acrid and sour smoke lingering around them —the aftermath of their shots—and the victory that came with it.

"But …" Then Gilbert raised his hands, along with his pistol.

Jean stepped into the cabin and snatched the pistol. A large red stain was emanating from the thigh of the man beside Gilbert. The man stumbled and fell, and the thump vibrated in Jean's heart. He hated seeing people suffer, which is why he avoided violence at all costs. He tossed his musket and the pistol to Whiteman, then leaped to the fallen man, ripped a piece of his shirt and bound it around the man's thigh above the wound. Gilbert's ashen face appeared beside Jean, and his voice was hoarse. "This is Mr. Randall."

"Whiteman, fetch a wide—*mon Dieu*. Scott, you are bleeding from your head."

Scott nodded and brushed across the shiny red with a grin. "Winged me with buckshot, is all."

Jean shot Gilbert a darting glance. "Buckshot?" Then he shook his head, mumbling that even Cosma used proper munition, and puffed. "*Donc*, Whiteman, fetch me a wide log. Scott, you're coming with me. The others will haul the keelboat back to Gaudins's."

Mr. Randall opened his eyes and tried to sit up, and Jean held him down by the shoulder. "It's all right, Mr. Randall. I will bring you to a physician." The injured man glanced at inspector Gilbert, who nodded.

Though the attack was over, Jean's heart still beat with its thrill. He would only know his profit once he had paid everyone and sold the leftover goods. But his triumph was not only the retrieved merchandise, it was something far more personal. He had managed, despite all odds, to give

Gilbert a lesson of a lifetime—that Jean was not a heartless marauder, or a scoundrel, to put it in Gilbert's words, but a fair man if one cooperated. A gentleman, if you will.

The men did as instructed and soon Jean carried one end of the plank they had tied Mr. Randall to—to prevent him slipping off—and Scott the other. Its weight dug into Jean's right shoulder, and the man on it twitched from fear of falling. With every movement, the wood forced its way into Jean's bone, firing a shock through his arm.

"I'm grate—" Jean's voice broke, and he cleared his throat to summon it. "Grateful—truly—for your commitment, Scott. I will reimburse you for the wounds you suffered."

"Oh—you should thank the biddy."

"The what?"

Scott chortled, and Jean could feel the vibration in his shoulder. "As we neared the keelboat, a chicken fell into the river. Gilbert's men didn't realize what we were after and urged us to retrieve it for them. We did, disguising our guns, and then mounted the keelboat with ease."

Jean laughed, and the tied-up Mr. Randall scoffed. "Very well. Our crew is growing more diverse by the day." With his focus on the house uphill, Jean shifted the log on his shoulder, and Randall gasped at the movement. "First a mulatto, then a woman, now a feathered associate ..."

CHAPTER 8
A WOLF NO MORE

After he dropped off pale-faced Mr. Randall at Gaudins's house, Jean borrowed a horse and fetched a physician.

"You're in luck, Mr. Randall," said the physician. "The wound is not as bad as it looks."

Parched from the struggle of carrying first Cosma and then Randall up the hill, Jean left the room to find water, and when he returned, saw Gilbert whispering to the doctor through the slanted door. "... the strangest vision, doctor ... right before the attack. A Fata Morgana, I suppose."

"You lost a lot today. It's the stress, Inspector, we are not in the desert."

Jean puffed, knocked and pushed the creaking door open. "I'll help you bring Randall to a nearby house for recovery." Gilbert looked up with a tense face, then nodded, and soon after, Gilbert and his men left, allowing Jean to return to Scott, whom he found recovering with every sip.

Jean joined his men to celebrate. They paraded the chicken in the garden, honoring its feat with singing so discordant Jean wasn't sure they even sang the same shanty. Did he hear the religious hymn he remembered from church prayers in Bordeaux—*The Admiral of The Ocean Sea*—which was, for being a song everyone knew from church, often sung on ships? Except that they replaced 'sweet virgin Mary' with 'sweet virgin biddy'. Then Jean saw Whiteman return the chicken to its den and remembered Cosma. He stumbled and held onto a tree to catch his breath, grabbed food and a drink, and knocked on her guest room door.

"Aye." Cosma's voice was husky.

Jean opened and saw a faint flash of her teeth in the darkness. He placed the dinner on the mattress, spilling wine, and stumbled to the door. "Lemme get a candle."

"Stay," said Cosma. "I don't need a candle. How do ye dry a pistol?" She threw it on the bed. "It got wet."

Jean held onto the door's cool metal lock, nodded and left it slanted, for the room had a musky odor of sweat. Then he sat beside her, opened the Queen Anne and laid it to the side. "Let it sit till tomorrow. How's your condition?"

Cosma removed the thin linen, exposing the outline of a swollen leg. Jean grimaced. "What did the doctor say?"

Cosma looked away. "Wouldn't treat it because I'm an adventuress."

Jean's jaw slacked, and he glared out the slant in the door. He had gone to celebrate rather than check on Cosma. "I should have taken care of you."

The garden party passed by the window, singing, "O clement, O loving, O sweet virgin biddy ..."

Cosma shrugged. "Ye had other business."

"I apologize," Jean said and took her hands in his, and noticing how cold they were, kissed them. A salty savor remained on his lips. "Why, your hand is wet."

In their regained confidence, the smugglers resumed to the pirate songs they sang on Barataria.

Cosma retrieved her arm, brushed it across her cheek and wiped it on her dress.

Jean's face grew hot. "What's the matter, mademoiselle?" He gazed into her eyes and placed his hand over hers.

Cosma sniffed and stared at her feet. "Why do they call it 'amorous congress'?"

"Huh?"

Cosma cocked her head at Jean, and even without light he could see the glimmer of tears. "It's hardly ever … amorous."

"Are you worried about your leg?" Jean held onto her hands. "I will see you recover. You needn't work in the meantime."

"Ye said intimacy was a weapon." Cosma took a deep breath that quivered as she exhaled. "I knew since I was a wee child, ye know. Since the first time someone forced me. Women can't gain enjoyment from force." She clenched her jaw and stared past Jean. "But they have other weapons, and as any man, I shall use them."

Jean gaped, forming airless words, then swallowed them. "Did someone force you today?" He moved close to her face to see better, met with a sweet-metallic scent, and got up.

"Don't," Cosma said, but Jean ignored her and left the room.

He plucked a candle from the dining table, a serviette and a bottle of brandy, and when he opened the door to Cosma, he gasped. Half her face was dark with bruises, her lip burst but not yet swollen. "Who did this to you?"

Cosma turned away, hiding the bruised side of her face. "It's none of yer concern."

"I protect my men, and so shall I you." He paced the small room, causing the flame to flicker.

"Then stay with me." Cosma's hand reached for his feet, but the cloth of his breeches slipped between her fingers as he moved away. "Help me forget it."

Jean put the candle beside the bed and kneeled, poured brandy on the serviette and wiped the blood away. His shoulders were heavy with grief, and he wished he could wipe away her fears along with the blood. He gave her clean but swelling face a pitiful inspection. "How?"

"Bed me."

"I ..." Jean strode to the other end of the room and caressed the wood of a horizontal beam in the door. "I can't. It's not proper, mademoiselle. It's the last thing you need. You must get your mind off ..." His nails dug into the soft wood.

"Am I living in my body or are ye?" Cosma's voice filled with reproach. "It's not the first time, Jean. And I know what helps me."

He shook his head and sat beside her on the mattress. In her matte eyes, he read resentment, fatigue, and restlessness. "But your leg. You are in no cond—"

"Touch it." Cosma moved the linen and the untouched food away. He lost himself in those eyes. She took his hand and placed it on her knee.

What could she gain from this? He couldn't conceive of an end that would serve her. Worried about hurting the bruised skin, he let the tips of his fingers run along her swollen shin. Goosebumps rose under his touch.

What was Cosma missing? Then he recalled she had

lost her mother. Without her, Cosma had no caring shoulder to ease her worries. Now she wanted a fresh memory to erase the aggression impressed on her soft body.

Cosma closed her eyes. Her skin was tight under his fingers and imagining the pain she was in made his own tingle. He gently brushed across her still-damp cheek and felt his eyes swelling with tears of his own. How could anyone hurt a woman this way? With a pang, he realized his hand had wandered down the side of her neck, and she was stretching her head to let it proceed. He moved back up, but her hand caught his and placed his palm on her cleavage. It was sweaty and sandy, and he could feel the drumming of her heart against her rib cage. Then she pulled her corset down and her breasts swelled over its edge.

She wasn't afraid at all. She wanted control. To get back what had been taken from her. Then she took his other hand, spread her legs and lay it on her mossy mound. It was wet, glossy in the flickering candlelight. Afraid to hurt her, Jean let his hand glide across it, hardly touching her, at which she arched her back. "What's wrong? Are you in pain?"

She grunted. "No."

Cosma's behavior was new to him. Was this part of the voodoo she spoke of earlier? To mind came convulsing dancers around a fire. Jean had been with women before —French *filles de joie*, who flirted outrageously and squealed when loved properly. Also, he recalled a few ladies of high standing that fluttered their lashes and avoided eye contact. But Cosma was none of those things. She was driven by an enigmatic force—calm and irresistible—that possessed both her and her onlooker. He felt its heat reach through his hand, enter his skin and soothe him from within, then steal away his warning thoughts.

She clutched his breeches and tore them open. Was it right? He gasped as she pulled him close, and stumbled forward, crushing onto her. As he pushed himself up, she locked her bright eyes on his and didn't let go of her grip on his shirt, guiding him. He gasped again. Seeing her convulse, he retracted, but she grabbed his hips and yanked him down.

He tried to tear away. "It's hurting you."

"No." Cosma forced him down, and Jean let the possession own him and ride them both. She arched under him, and Jean kissed her neck, traveling down and at last savoring her earthly taste. She was like a wolf—untamable and fierce, and yet an intricate part of nature—a balancing act in itself, forcing you to see all, good and bad. What he grudged when concerned with privateering—her powerful emotions and spurting actions—he loved now. Her voiceless scream ended in a limp smile as she drew him close again, driving him over the edge. He stared into her amber eyes, one smaller than the other for the bulging on her face. He caught a cool tear escaping pain with the tip of his finger, then kissed her forehead, her nose, her lips ... then sat up. Was she smiling? With the swelling, it was impossible to tell. Perhaps he had hurt her. Cosma certainly looked worse for what he had done.

"I apologize, Madame."

Cosma let a sound escape her full lips that reminded of a snicker. "It is I who should apologize, Fita." Her voice was gentle, a side new to Jean. She opened her eyes and turned onto her side.

"Nonsense," he said.

"So ye'll keep me on ye crew?"

His jaw slacked. "You're highly irregular for a woman." He fixed his breeches.

Cosma had a glassy stare locked on him. "Maybe me ambitions are turning me into a man."

He stifled a snicker. "Fortunately, you are still missing a technicality there …"

"Huh?"

"Nothing."

"Ye're a true gentleman, Fita."

He gazed at her swollen leg and bruised face. "I'm uncertain."

Cosma cast him a crooked smile. "Nonsense. Now I need me a proper pirate name."

He took her hands and kissed them. To his satisfaction, they were warm now, and her eyes shone with excitement rather than resentment, despite her swelling. "Cosma Wolfe suits you well, I must admit."

"I want to leave Cosma Wolfe in the past." She retrieved her hand and pushed herself up. "It's me mother's name, and she's no longer. How would ye describe me?"

Jean's gaze traveled across her fizzy hair, dirty dress and muscled legs. "You have an initial striking beauty that your raw character quickly diminishes." Then he observed the glossy wax of the candle as it broke the thin wax wall and poured onto the candleholder. "If one doesn't know you."

"Aye," Cosma gave him a court nod. "Because I'm an adventuress."

He inhaled and turned to her with knotted brows. "I prefer a woman to have a cultivated character. And yet …" He waved his head and sighed. "I cannot explain it, Madame. *Vous êtez un intrigante méduse …*"

"What does *intrigante* mean?" Cosma gave the foreign word a pronunciation of her own making.

"Someone very …" His palm brushed over her thigh. "Intriguing. Attractive."

"Oh—oh. Like … Jezebel?"

"Not quite—"

"Aye, I like it." Cosma spread her fingers and moved them as if across the horizon. "They will call me the Jezebel Medusa."

NOTE TO THE READER

Inspector Walker Gilbert did exist, but he was only a customs inspector in Donaldsonville and not a detective, and his character traits are completely fictional. I assume he was a respectable person in reality. Being the perfect antagonist, he served as a villain in this fictional story.

Claiborne, Jean Laffite, Pierre Laffite, Flaubert, Gaudins, Whiteman, all existed, and I stayed as close to historical sources as suited the story.

Cosma is entirely fictional, as is her mother.

Enjoyed this novelette? You could continue with The Ocean's Calling which is the next in series, or A Half Flower where characters of another story meet Jezebel a decade from the time of this novelette. If you would like to know more about Cosma's mother and how she ended up in Gallatin street, why not read the short story What Happened in the Marshlands?

All available at www.mira-kanehl.com.

FREE STARTER LIBRARY

Your honest review means a lot to me. A few words from you will shape my career as an independent author (because it will give other readers a chance to assess whether this book would interest them or not). Besides, I would really love to hear your thoughts on the story!

Get your FREE Mira Kanehl starter library

(See www.mira-kanehl.com)

You can unsubscribe at any time, but if you remain in the newsletter, you will be notified when new ones are published and sent links for free downloads where applicable.

If you have any questions or suggestions, I'll be happy to hear from you at author@mira-kanehl.com

ABOUT THE AUTHOR

Mirà Kanehl was born in Munich and raised in South India, a place where simplicity ruled a sunny life brimming with freedom and danger. She spent her youth climbing trees, swimming in pools and the ocean, riding ponies and horses, reading, compulsory daily sports of all kinds and later ballet training. Stories and books were her passion from the days before school, when life was simple.

It wasn't that she decided one day she'd try become an author, the question never occurred to her. She always wrote. But one New Years she decided this would be the year she would write a full book and publish it. She did.

As with many indie authors, sales were slow and she didn't enjoy the marketing aspect, which mirrored in sales. She took a break but couldn't stop writing, and after a few years (and having written more books) realized being a full-time author is all she ever dreamed of. Now she splits her time writing and marketing, composing book reviews for readers of her genre, and building a living from her passion.

Learn more about her at www.mira-kanehl.com.

ALSO BY MIRÀ KANEHL

Naupaka Series:

A Half Flower

A young French doctor involved in the aftershocks of the French Revolution flees to Hawaii and steps into the next political debate. It may be his last.

One Virtue and a Thousand Crimes Series:

What Happened in the Marshlands

1811, short-story

Amid dust whirled up by drumming footsteps of the slave revolt, Ayida fears for the future of her daughter.

The Adventuress

1813, novelette

Smuggler Jean Laffite meets a stunning woman that may be the demise to his business.

The Ocean's Calling

1813, novel

Many women of her time want protection or freedom. Cosma wants to be a pirate.

NOTE TO THE REVIEWER

I am grateful for your review! Here are some questions that might help:

What happened in the book?

Which character did you connect with, and why?

Did the story pull you in?

How did it make you feel?

When and where was the turning point or top of the story arc? (Try not to give spoilers, or please give a spoiler alert.)

Was there a point where you were confused about what was happening or why it was happening?

What other books would you compare this one to?

How would you describe the writing style, and did it remind you of any other author you've read?

Senses make the strongest memories. Which of your senses did the story most trigger? Did characters eat? Touch? Smell? See? Hear?

Would you recommend the book to your best friend with similar book interests?

Explain the book in one sentence (it's more difficult than it sounds!).

~

If you have any questions or suggestions, I'll be happy to hear from you at author@mira-kanehl.com.

If you want to add icing to the cupcake, why not take this short survey regarding this book and how it can be improved?

www.ingramcontent.com/pod-product-compliance
Lightning Source LLC
Chambersburg PA
CBHW020648160726
47991CB00003B/1086